cleveland architecture coloring book

illustrated by
Jeremy Smith
with   **Michael Abrahamson**
Theodore Ferringer
Austin Kotting
Allison Szalkowski

designbelt

#	Year	Building	Architect
1.	1912	*West Side Market*	Hubbell and Benes
2.	1929	*Terminal Tower*	Graham, Anderson, Probst & White
3.	1948	*Greyhound Bus Terminal*	William Strudwick Arrasmith
4.	1953	*Park Synagogue*	Erich Mendelsohn
5.	1953	*Peter Lloyd Residence*	Ernst Payer
6.	1955	*Louis Penfield Residence*	Frank Lloyd Wright
7.	1958	*55 Public Square*	Carson, Lundin, and Shaw
8.	1959	*ASM International World Headquarters*	John Terence Kelly and R. Buckminster Fuller
9.	1962	*Wade Commons*	Outcalt, Guenther, Rode & Bonebrake
10.	1965	*Pier W.*	Stouffer Corporation
11.	1966	*James F. Lincoln Library*	Victor Christ-Janer
12.	1968	*Tower East*	The Architects' Collaborative
13.	1971	*Cleveland Meseum of Art, Education Wing*	Marcel Breuer and Associates
14.	1971	*Ameritrust Tower*	Marcel Breuer and Associates
15.	1974	*University Center*	Don Hisaka
16.	1985	*Crile Building*	Cesar Pelli
17.	1995	*Rock and Roll Hall of Fame and Museum*	I. M. Pei
18.	2002	*Peter B. Lewis Weatherhead School of Management*	Frank Gehry
19.	2003	*Ceruti House*	Thom Stauffer
20.	2005	*Corporate College East*	URS Corporation
21.	2007	*Akron Art Museum*	Coop Himmelb(l)au
22.	2008	*C-House*	Robert Maschke Architects
23.	2009	*Mintz Residence*	Robert Maschke Architects
24.	2010	*Hillcrest Hospital Expansion*	Westlake Reed Leskosky
25.	2010	*Bertram and Judith Kohl Building*	Westlake Reed Leskosky
26.	2010	*Bill Julka Hall*	NBBJ
27.	2011	*Cares Tower*	Cannon Design
28.	2011	*Seidman Cancer Center*	Cannon Design
29.	2012	*Uptown Cleveland*	Stanley Saitowitz / Natoma Architects
30.	2012	*Museum of Contemporary Art*	Farshid Moussavi Architecture

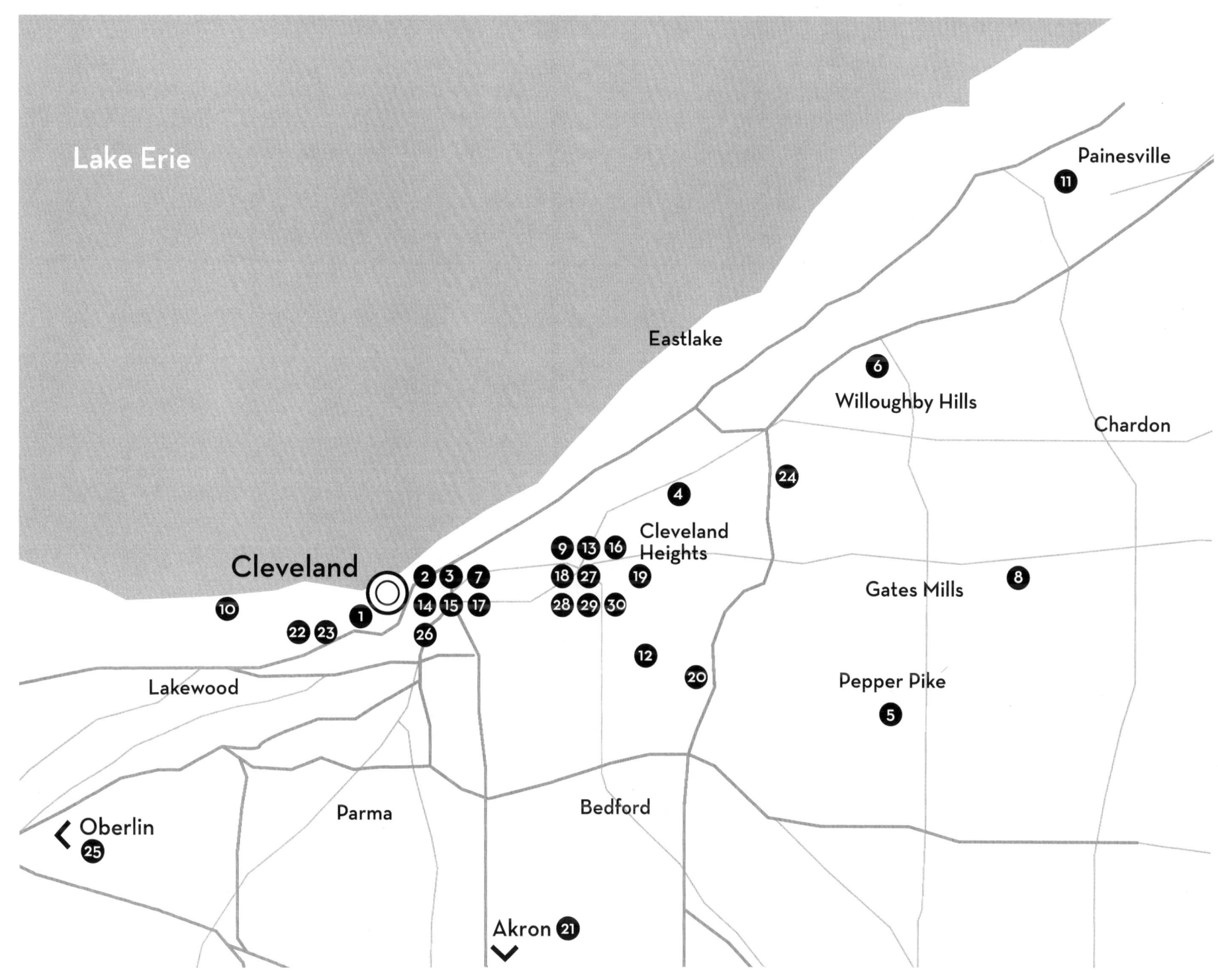

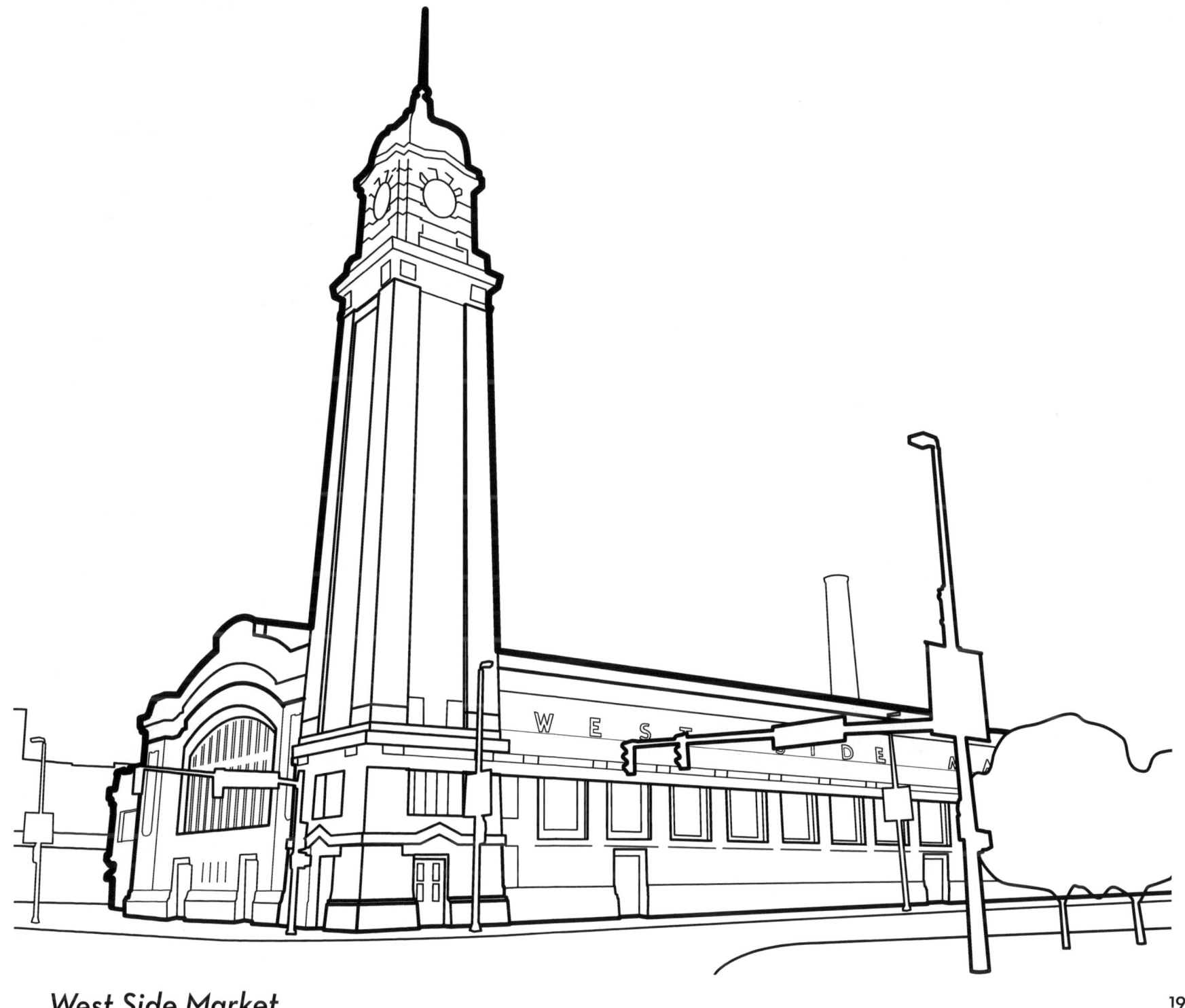

West Side Market
1979 West 25th Street   Cleveland, Ohio

1912
Hubbell and Benes

2 *Terminal Tower*
50 Public Square   Cleveland, Ohio

1929
Graham, Anderson, Probst & White

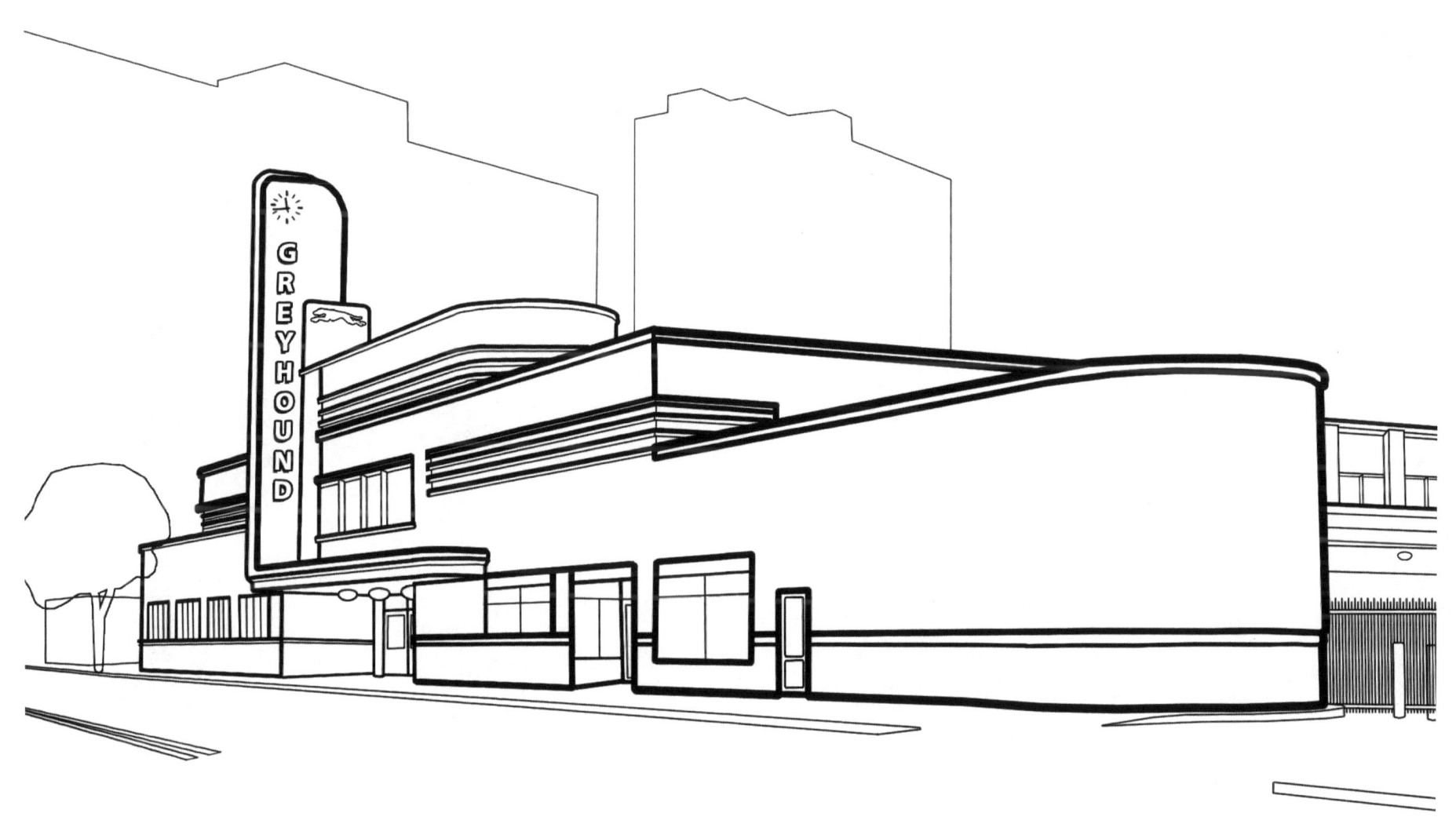

Greyhound Bus Terminal
3   1465 Chester Avenue   Cleveland, Ohio

1948
William Strudwick Arrasmith

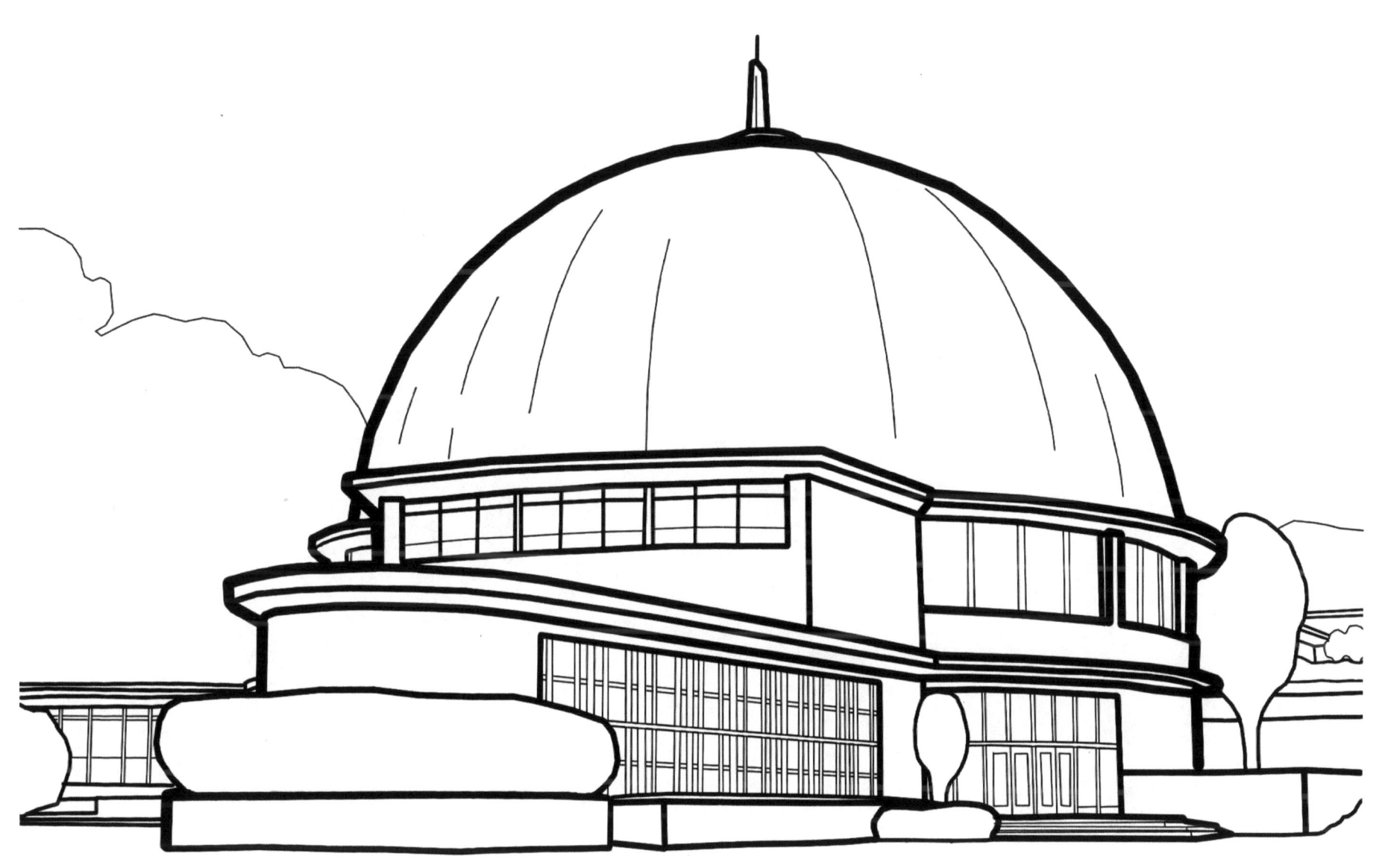

Park Synagogue
4 3300 Mayfield Road   Cleveland Heights, Ohio

1953
Erich Mendelsohn

Peter Lloyd Residence
Moreland Hills, Ohio (Demolished 2003)

1953
Ernst Payer

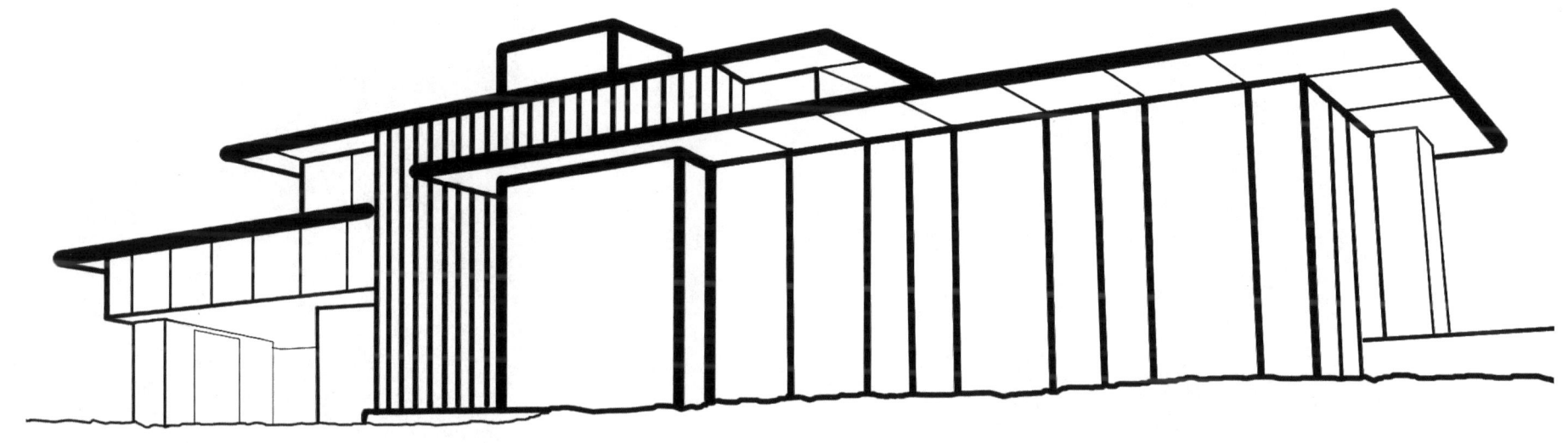

Louis Penfield Residence
6   2203 River Road   Willoughby Hills, Ohio

1955
Frankl Lloyd Wright

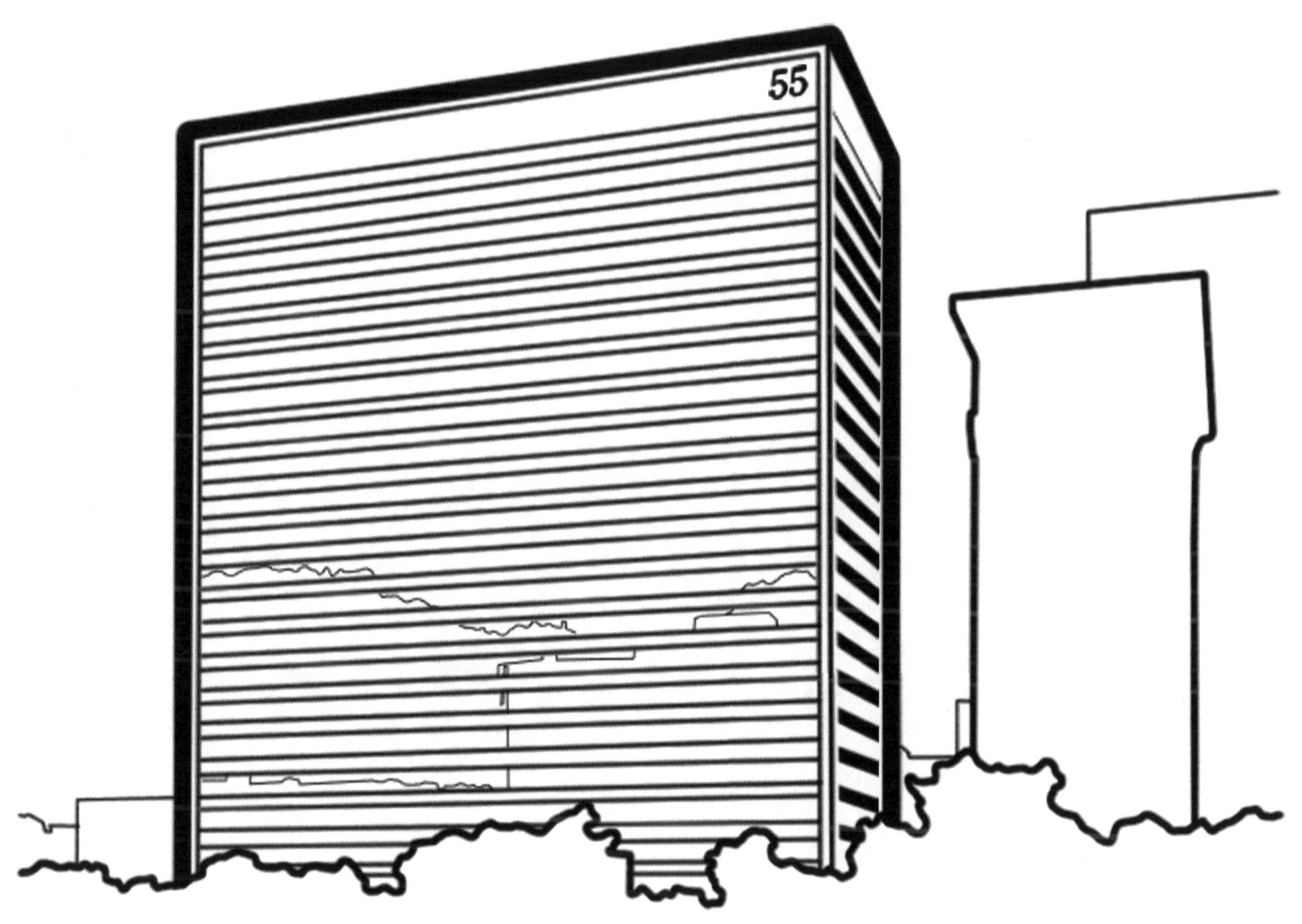

7 *55 Public Square*
55 Public Square   Cleveland, Ohio

1958
Carson, Lundin and Shaw

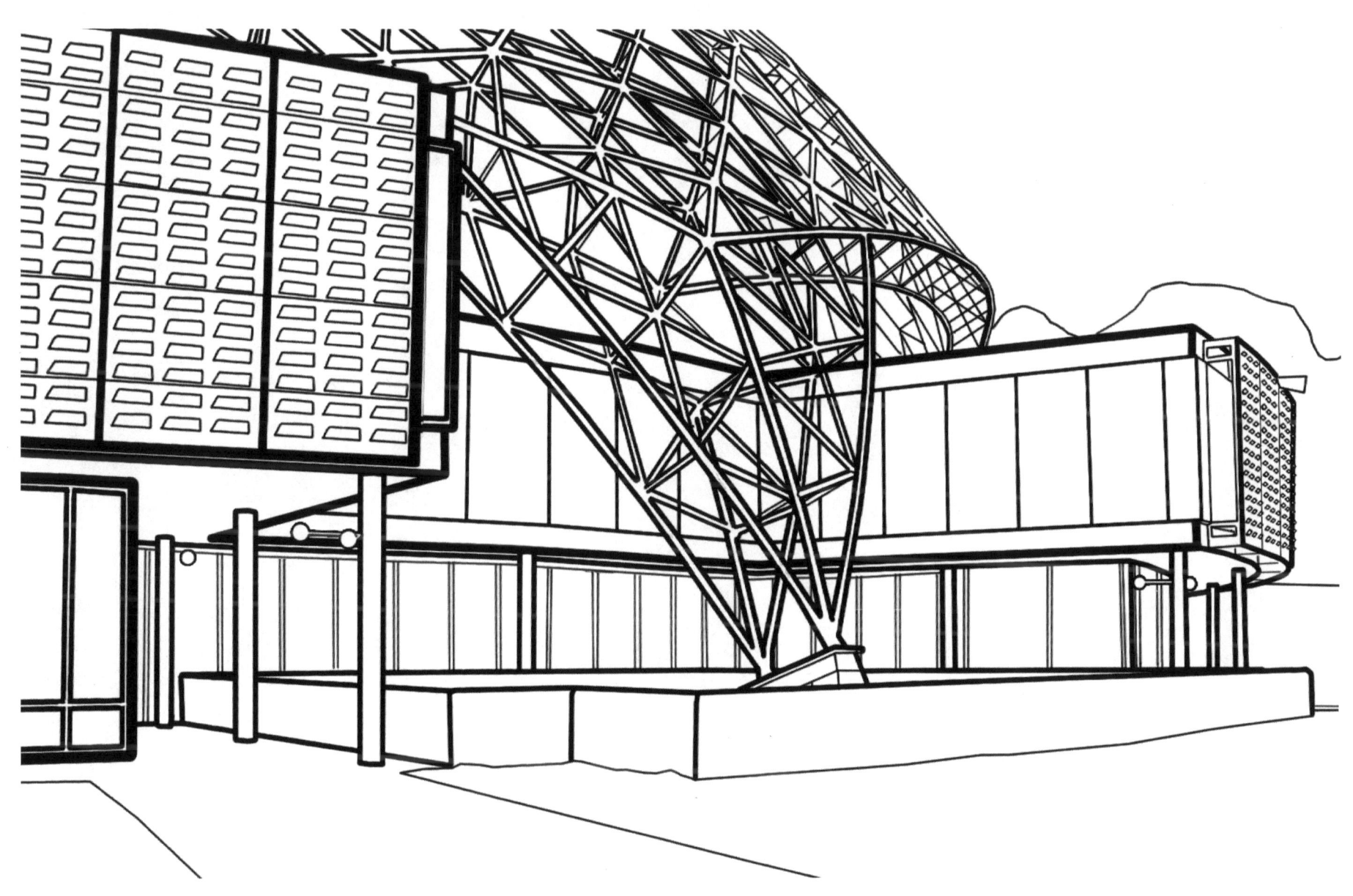

8 **ASM International World Headquarters**
9639 Kinsman Road   Novelty, Ohio

1959
John Terence Kelly and R. Buckminster Fuller

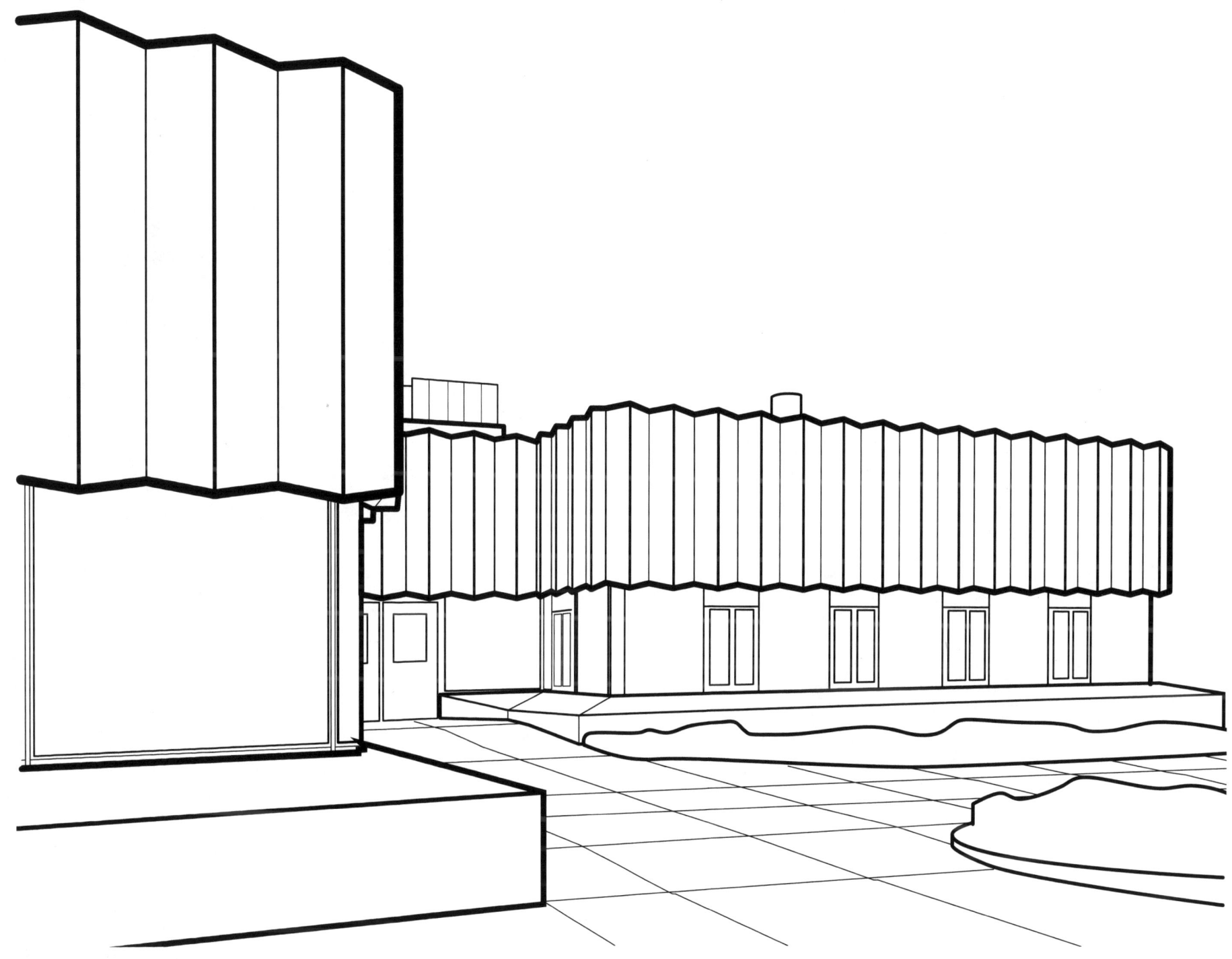

9 **Wade Commons** Case Western Reserve University   11451 Juniper Road   Cleveland, Ohio   Outcalt, Guetner, Rode & Bonebrake   1959

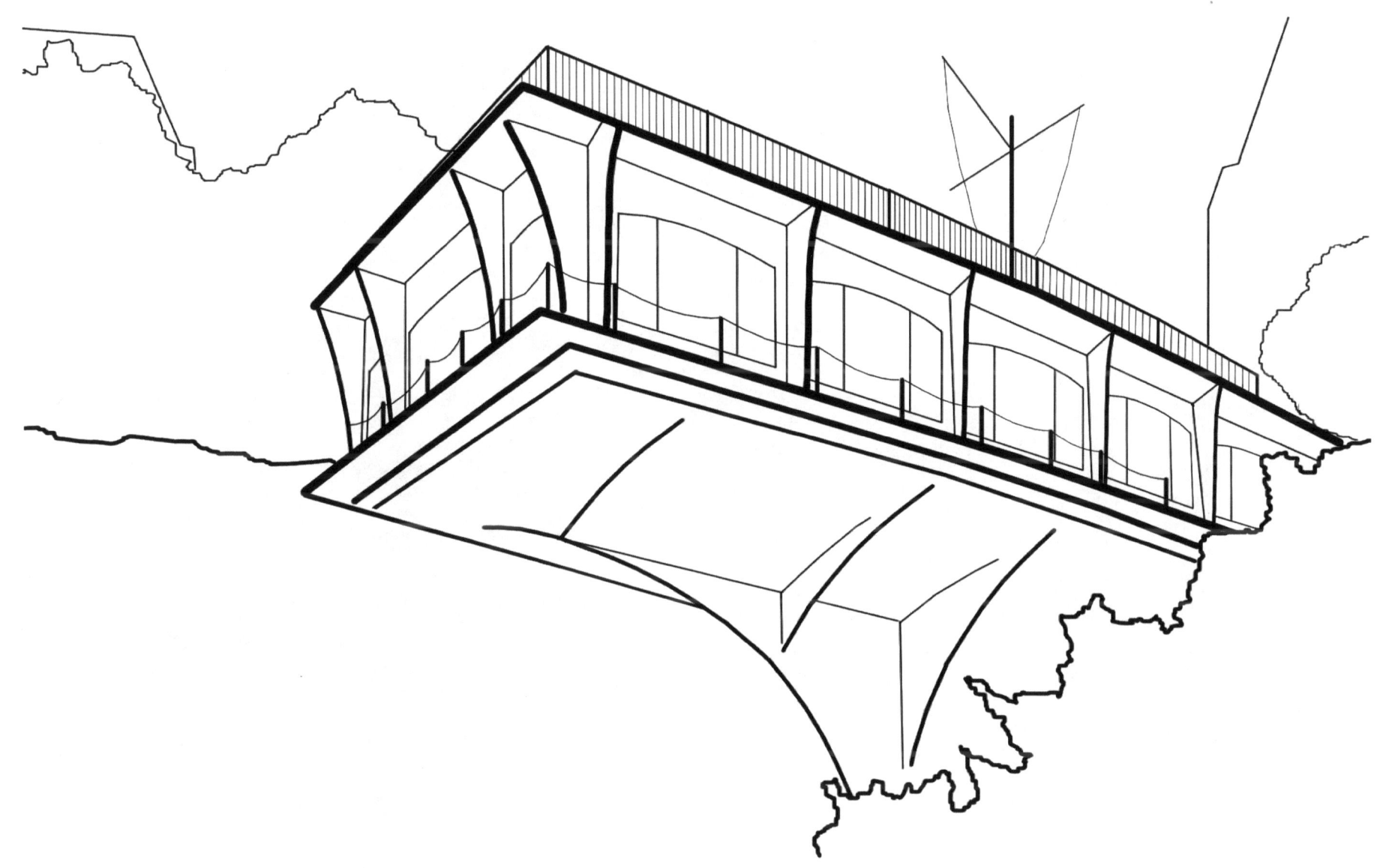

10 *Pier W.*
12700 Lake Avenue   Lakewood, Ohio

1965
Stouffer Corporation

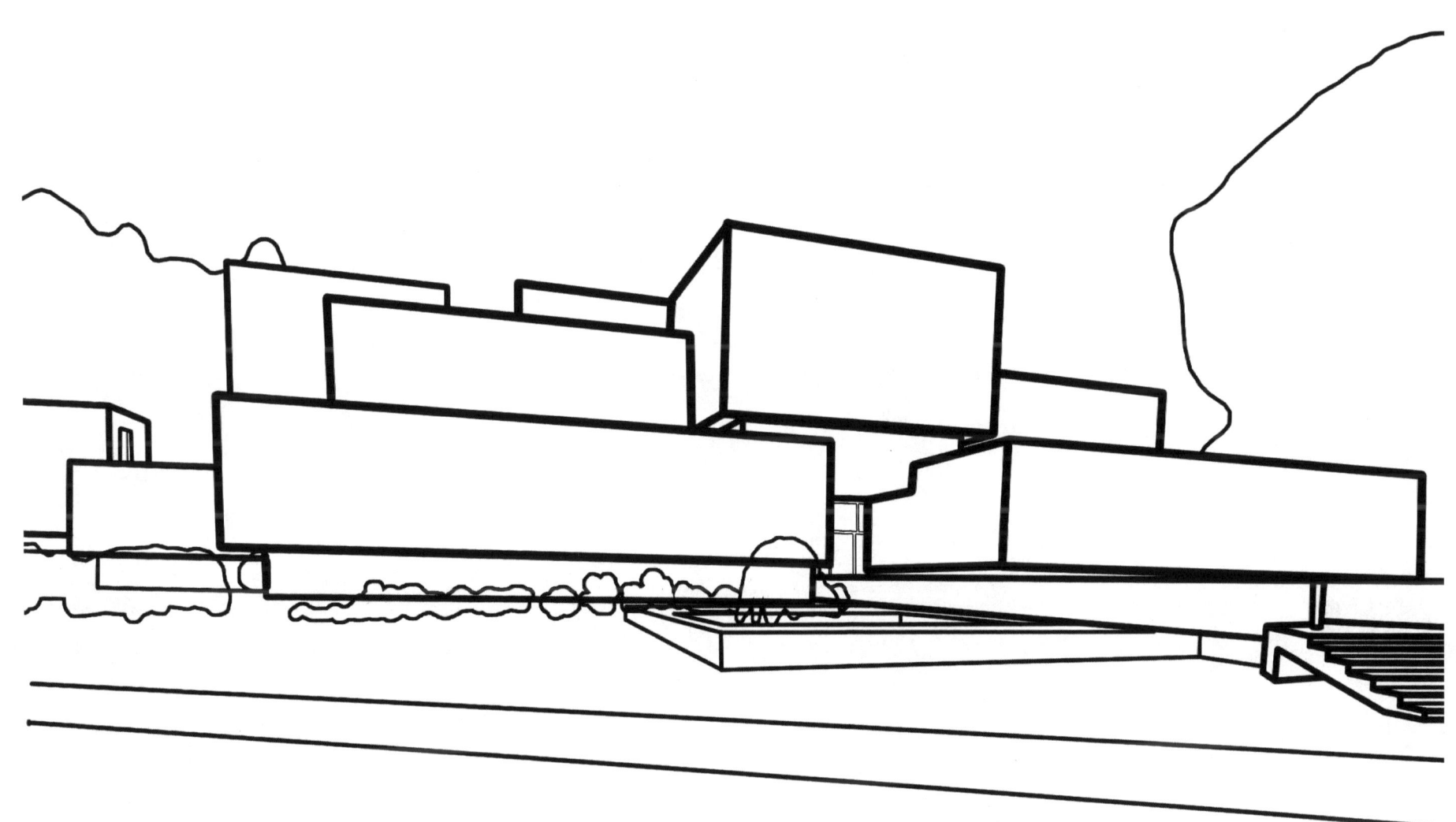

11 **James F. Lincoln Library**
Lake Erie College   391 West Washington Street   Painesville, Ohio

1966
Victor Christ-Janer

12 *Tower East* 20600 Chagrin Boulevard   Shaker Heights, Ohio

1968
The Architects' Collaborative

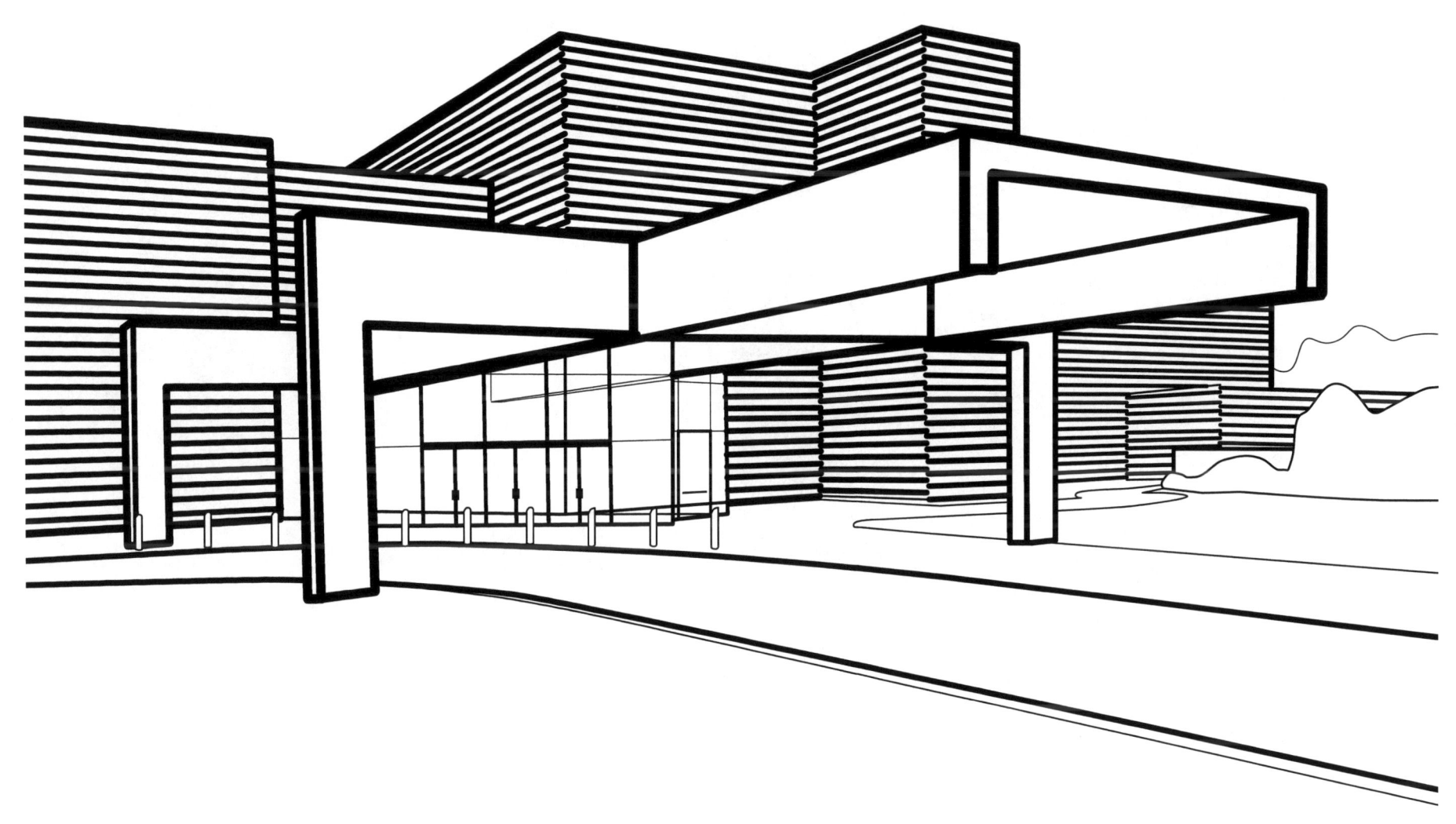

13 **Cleveland Museum of Art, Education Wing Expansion**
11150 East Boulevard   Cleveland, Ohio   (renovation, Rafael Viñoly Architects)

1971
Marcel Breuer and Associates

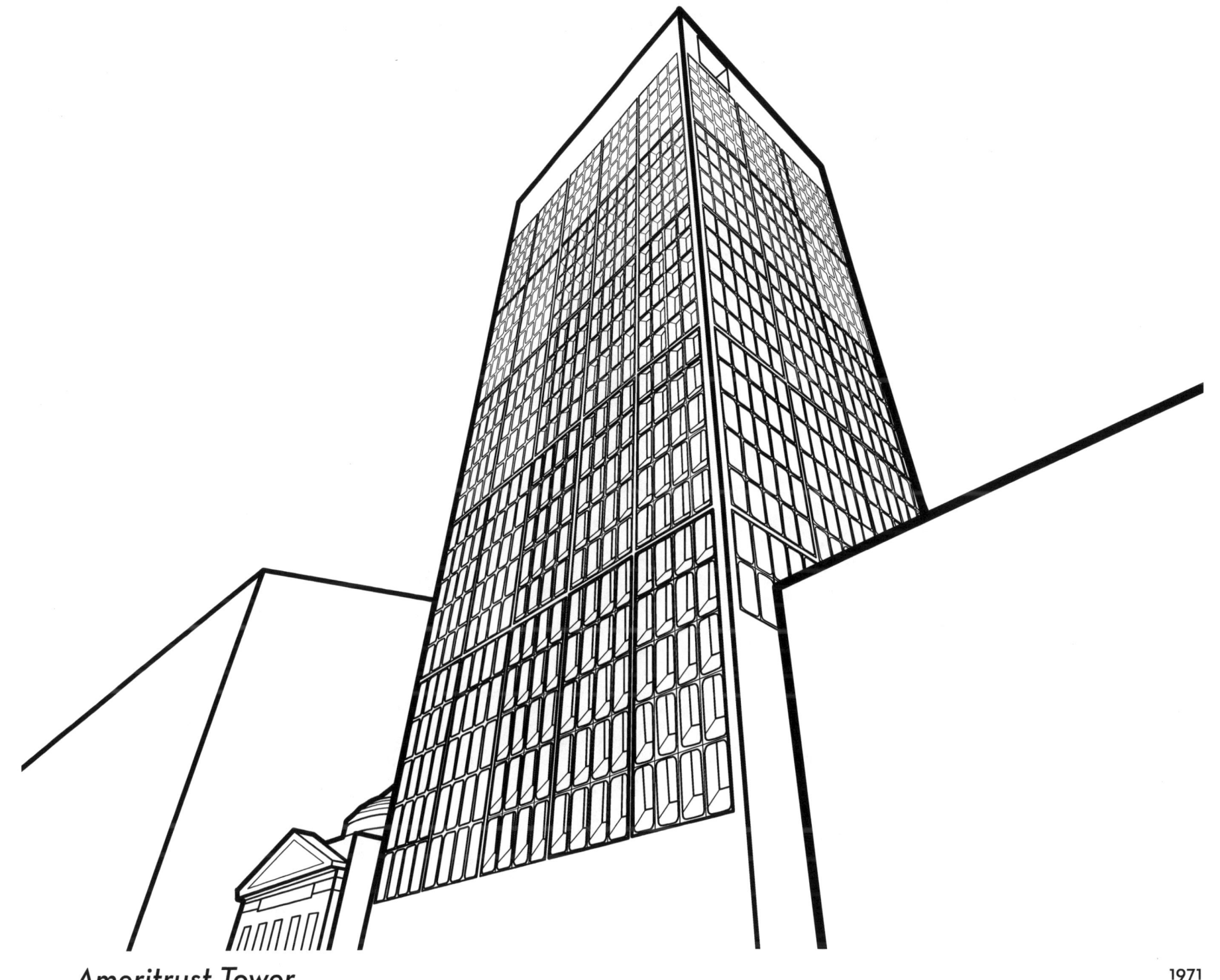

Ameritrust Tower
14 900 Euclid Avenue   Cleveland, Ohio

1971
Marcel Breuer and Associates

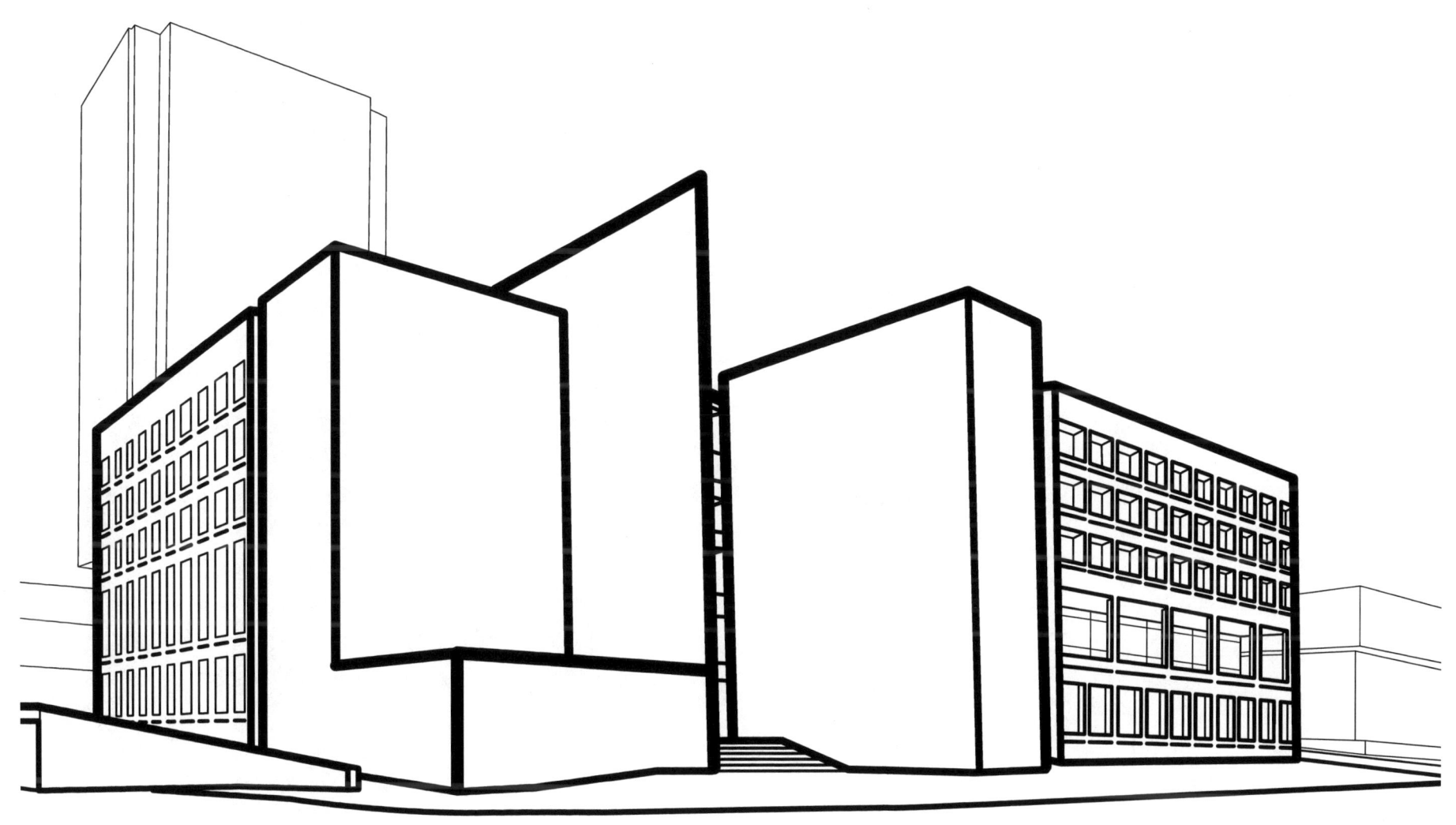

15 *University Center*
Cleveland State University   2121 Euclid Avenue   Cleveland, Ohio (Demolished 2009)

1974
Don Hisaka

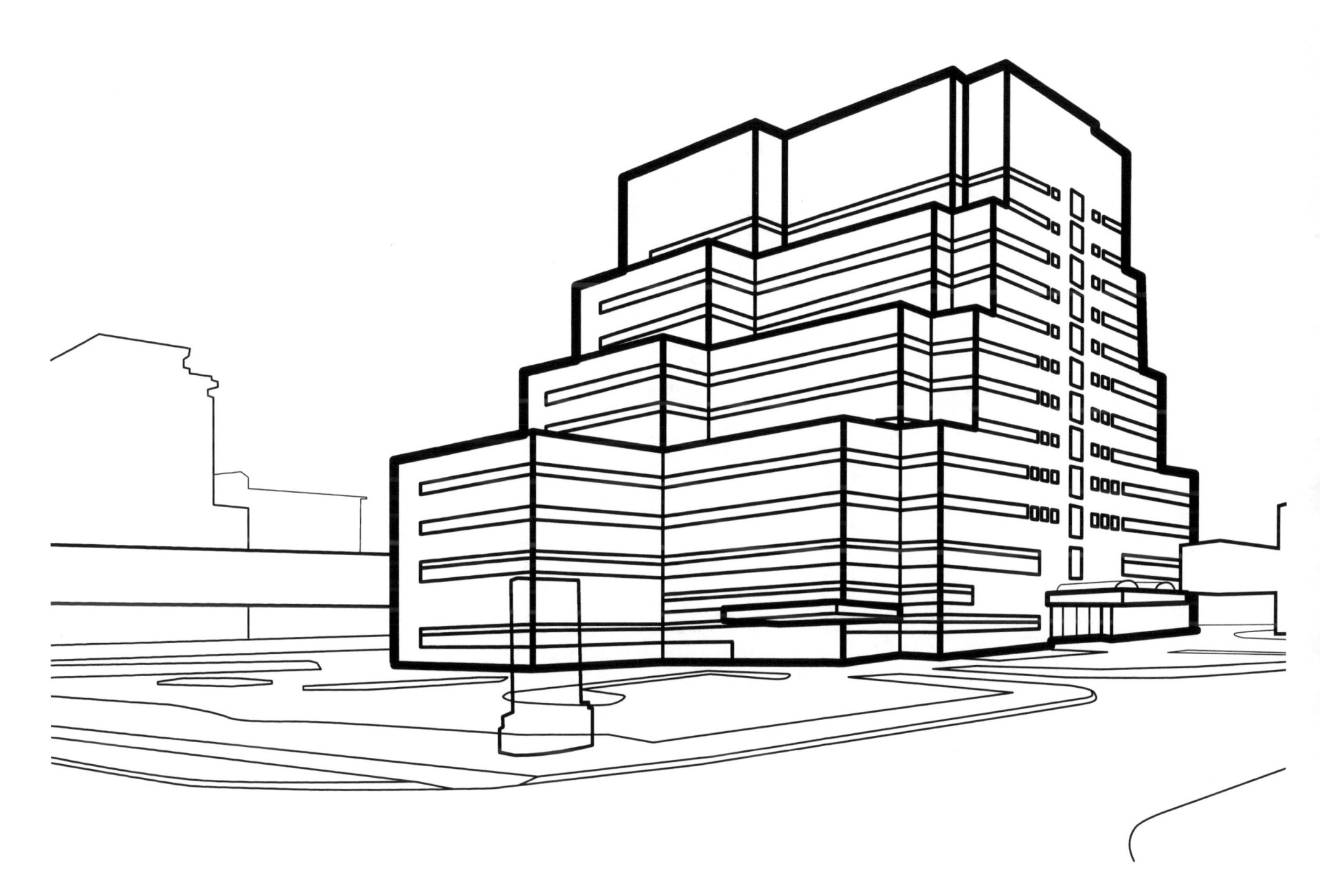

16 *Crile Building*
Cleveland Clinic Foundation   2049 East 100th Street   Cleveland, Ohio

1985
Cesar Pelli

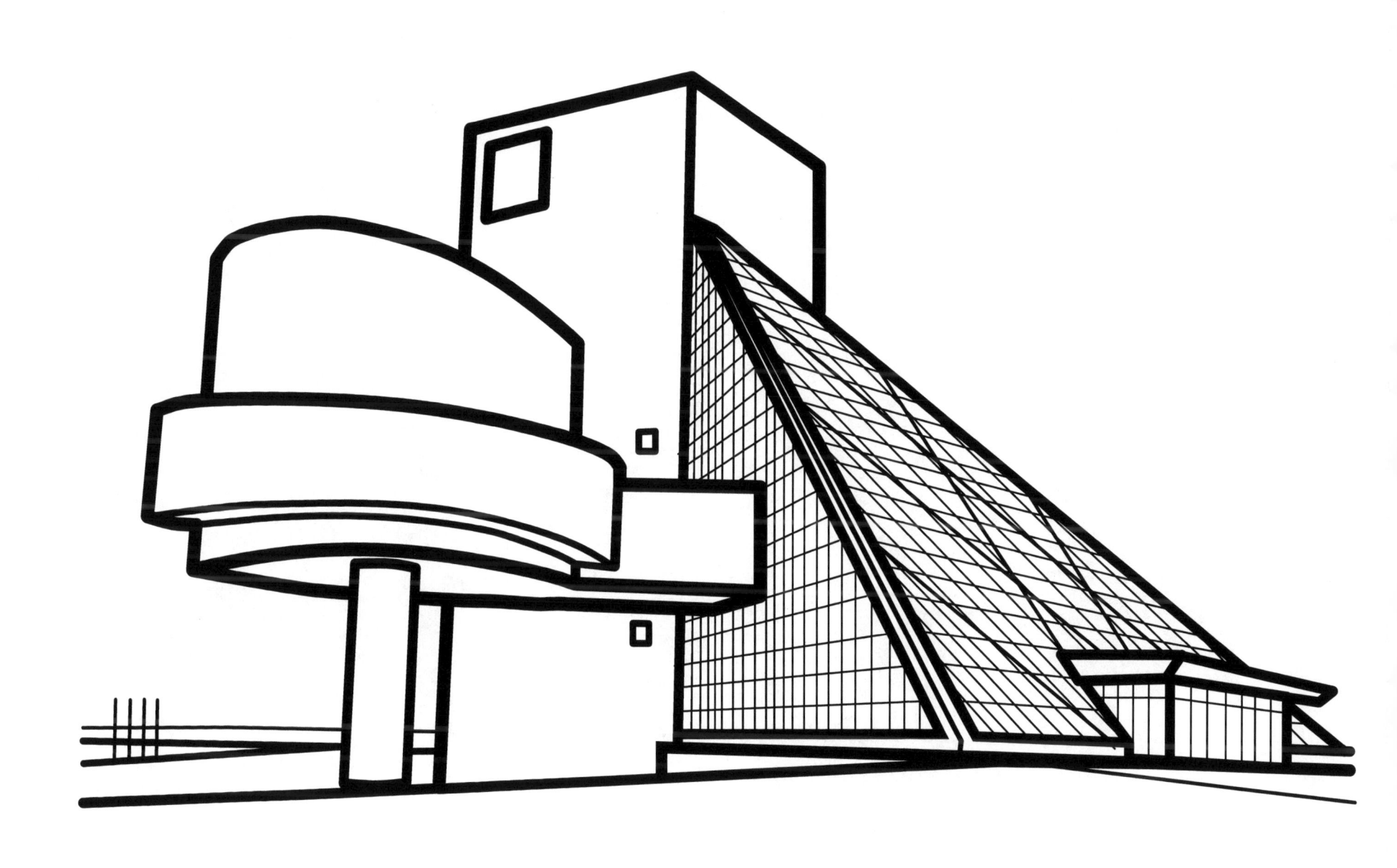

Rock and Roll Hall of Fame and Museum
17 751 Erieside Avenue Cleveland, Ohio

1995
I. M. Pei

18 **Peter B. Lewis Weatherhead School of Management**
Case Western Reserve University   11119 Bellflower Road   Cleveland, Ohio

2002
Frank Gehry

19 *Ceruti House*
Cleveland Heights, Ohio

2003
Thom Stauffer

Corporate College East

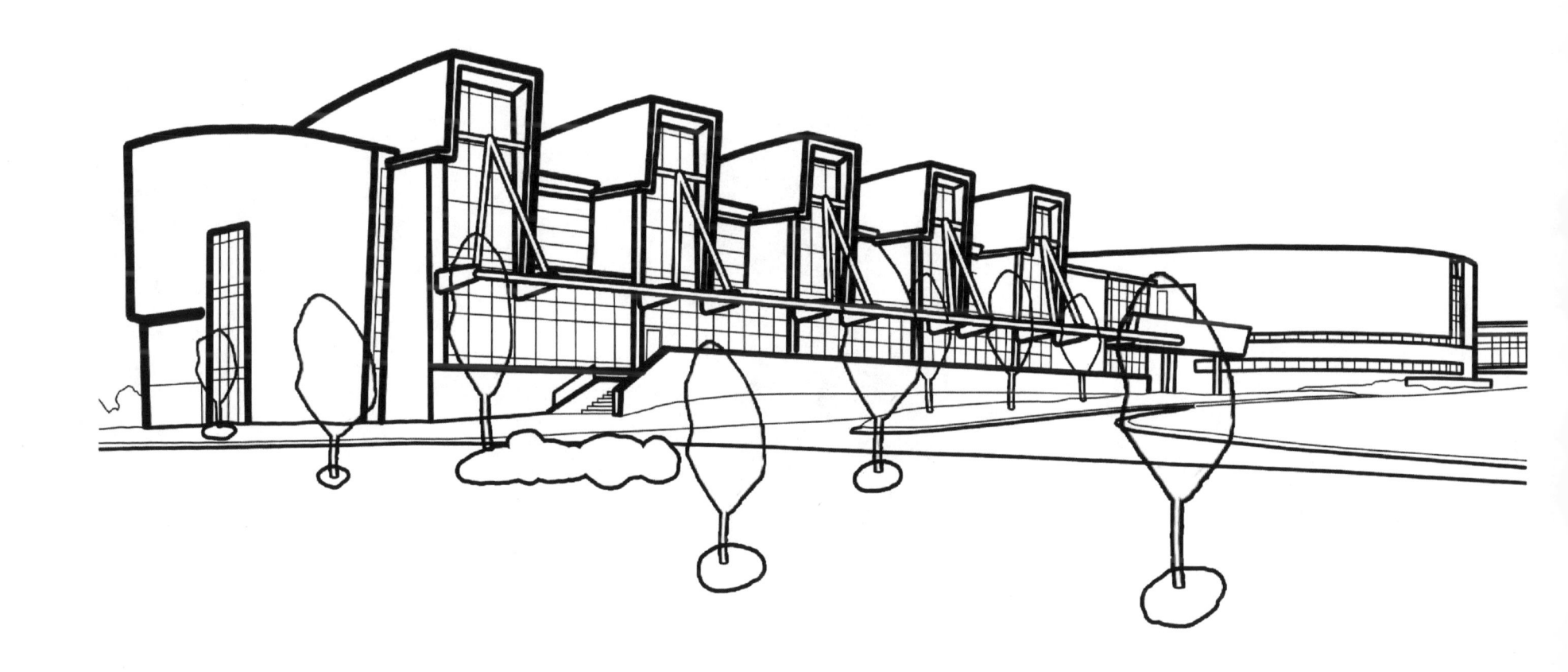

20 Cuyahoga Community College   4400 Richmond Road   Highland Hills, Ohio

2005
URS Corporation

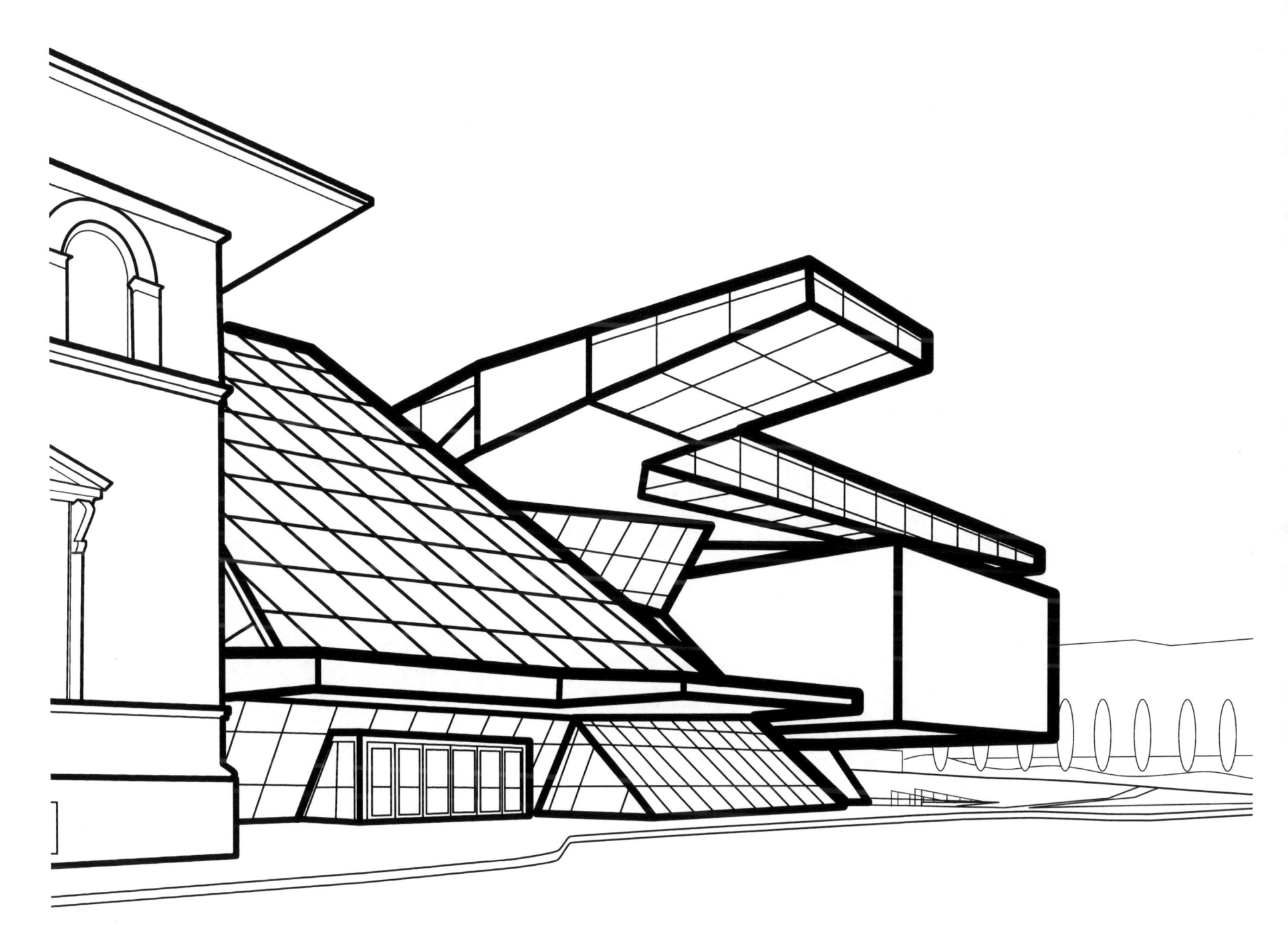

Akron Art Museum
21 1 South High Street Akron, Ohio

2007
Coop Himmelb(l)au

C House
Cleveland, Ohio

2008
Robert Maschke Architects

23 **Mintz Residence**
Cleveland, Ohio

2009
Robert Maschke Architects

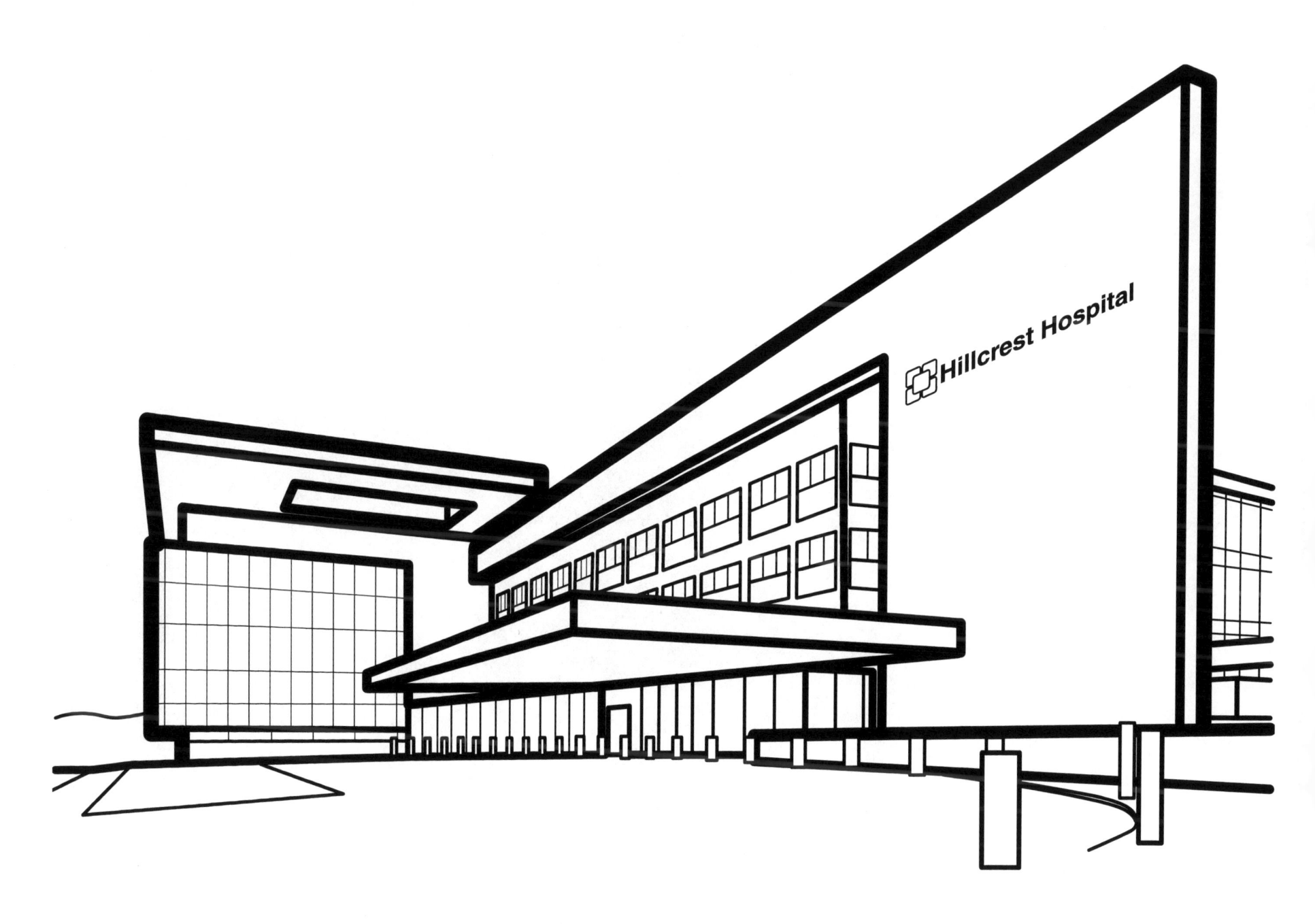

Hillcrest Hospital Expansion
Cleveland Clinic Foundation   6780 Mayfield Road   Mayfield Heights, Ohio

2010
Westlake, Reed, Leskosky

25 *Bertram and Judith Kohl Building*
Oberlin College   77 West College Street   Oberlin, Ohio

2010
Westlake, Reed, Leskosky

Bill Julka Hall
26 Cleveland State University   2121 Euclid Avenue   Cleveland, Ohio

2010
NBBJ

27 **Cares Tower**
U.S. Department of Veteran's Affairs   2121 Euclid Avenue   Cleveland, Ohio

2011
Cannon Design

28 *Seidman Cancer Center*
University Hospitals   11100 Euclid Avenue   Cleveland, Ohio

2011
Cannon Design

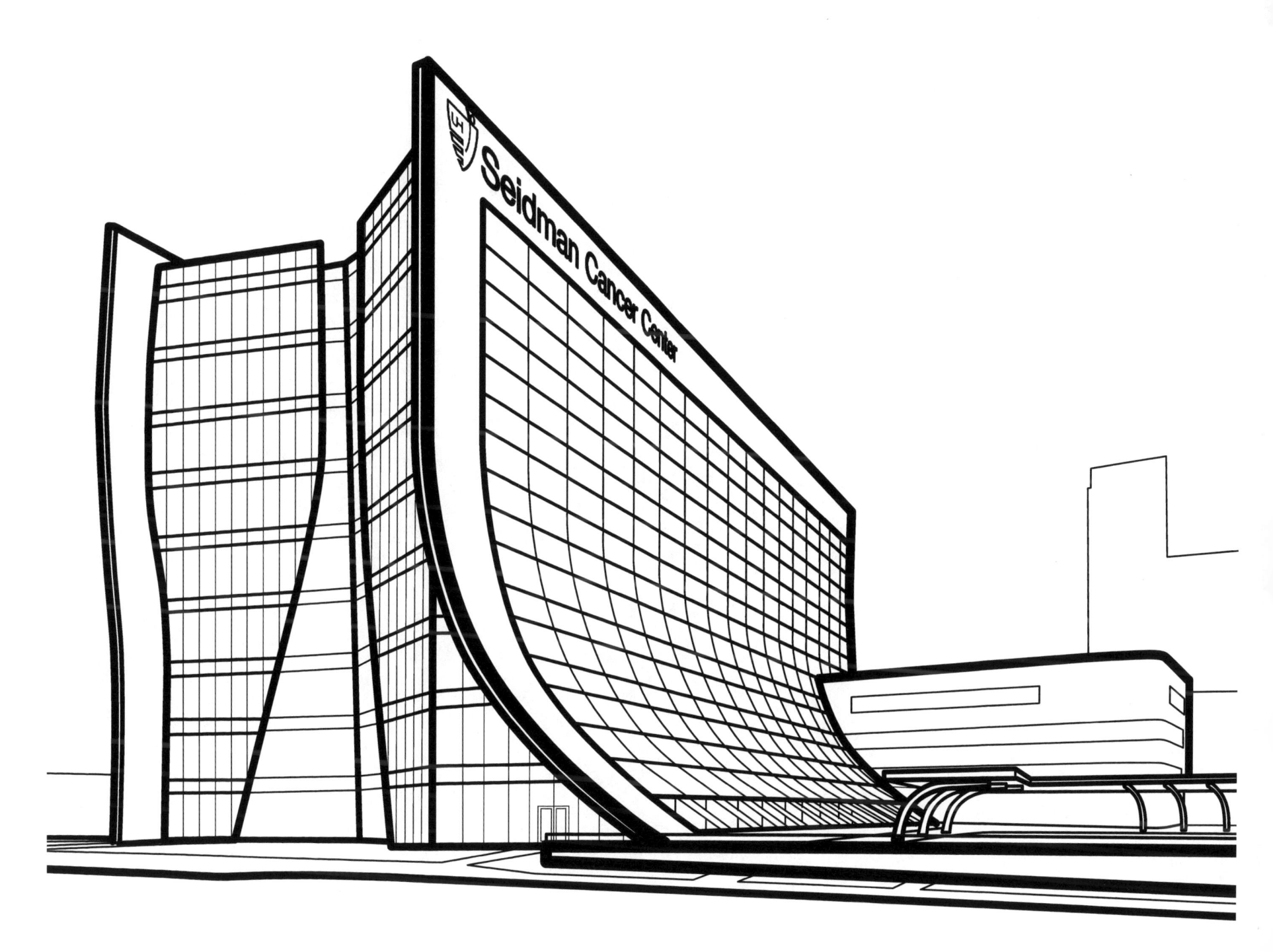

29 *Uptown Cleveland*
11490 Euclid Avenue   Cleveland, Ohio

2012
Stanley Saitowitz / Natoma Architects

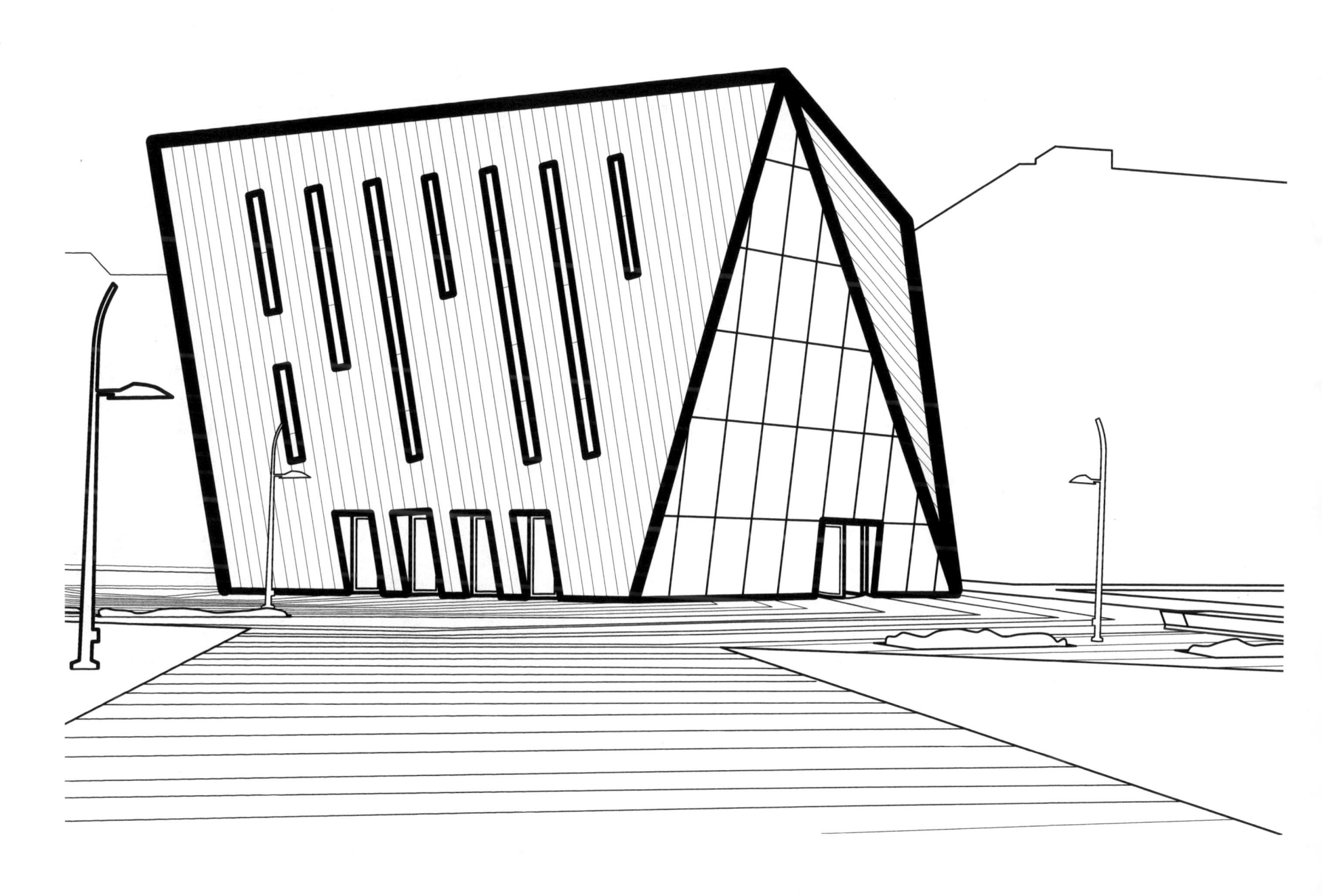

30 *Museum of Contemporary Art*
11400 Euclid Avenue   Cleveland, Ohio

2012
Farshid Moussavi Architecture

Published by
Designbelt
Jeremy Smith

©2012 Designbelt
All rights reserved
Printed and bound in Cleveland, Ohio
ISBN 978 1 4675 5495 4 Second Edition

No part of this book may be used or reproduced in any manner without written permission from the publisher, except in the context of reviews.

Creator, illustrator and editor
Jeremy Smith

Collaborators:
Michael Abrahamson
Theodore Ferringer
Austin Kotting
Allison Szalkowski

Disclaimer:
All credit for projects included in the Cleveland Architecture Coloring Book belongs to the architects, associated firms, and institutions identified. If any projects have not been identified properly, please notify the author, and a formal acknowledgement and correction will be issued in future editions.

Contact:
Designbelt, Jeremy Smith
jeremy@designbelt.mygbiz.com
designbelt.tumblr.com

This book is dedicated to my wife, Kate, for her endless love and support for the project and my career, as well as her ability to help edit and organize while focusing on her own career and ambitions; to my parents Marybeth and Gary, for their unwavering support and providing an environment that fostered a passion for the Arts and design at a young age that led me to where I am today; to the rest of my friends and family for always supporting my work and ideas with an openness that always challenges, encourages, and nurtures.

Jeremy Smith is the creator, illustrator and editor of the Cleveland Architecture Coloring Book. Jeremy attended Kent State University where he received master's degrees in both architecture and urban design, providing him the opportunity to teach, and study abroad on multiple occasions. In the five years since graduating from the Cleveland Urban Design Collaborative Jeremy has designed, curated, lectured, and practiced on many levels with a focus on social responsibility and activation.

Designbelt was launched in October, 2012 by Jeremy Smith as the production and publishing start-up company for the Cleveland Architecture Coloring Book and many other unique opportunities. The company's range includes architecture coloring books, conceptual design, urban design, graphic representation and diagramming. Designbelt works with a focus on design and social responsibility at every scale.

Special thanks to:

Elvira DiStanti
Victor and Beverly Janezic
Everett and Sandy Pennington
Gary and Marybeth Smith
Jason and Brianna Smith

robert maschke
ARCHITECTS

AIA Cleveland

THE CLEVELAND MUSEUM OF ART

MOCA
MUSEUM OF CONTEMPORARY ART
CLEVELAND

PORATH Print Source
Your one source for anything printed